It's My Birthday!

by Ryan Meechan.
Illustrated by Asher Eastwood-Sotto

For Abigail, Isabelle, Noah, George & Jude

10% of the money that the Author receives for this story will be donated to Bliss UK, A leading UK charity for Babies born premature or sick. Thank you for supporting such a worthwhile cause.

The morning had finally arrived. Isabelle kicked off her bed sheets and leaped into the air.

Then she dashed down the stairs and burst into the living room where Mommy, Daddy, her younger brother Noah, and her baby twin brothers George and Jude sat waiting for her.

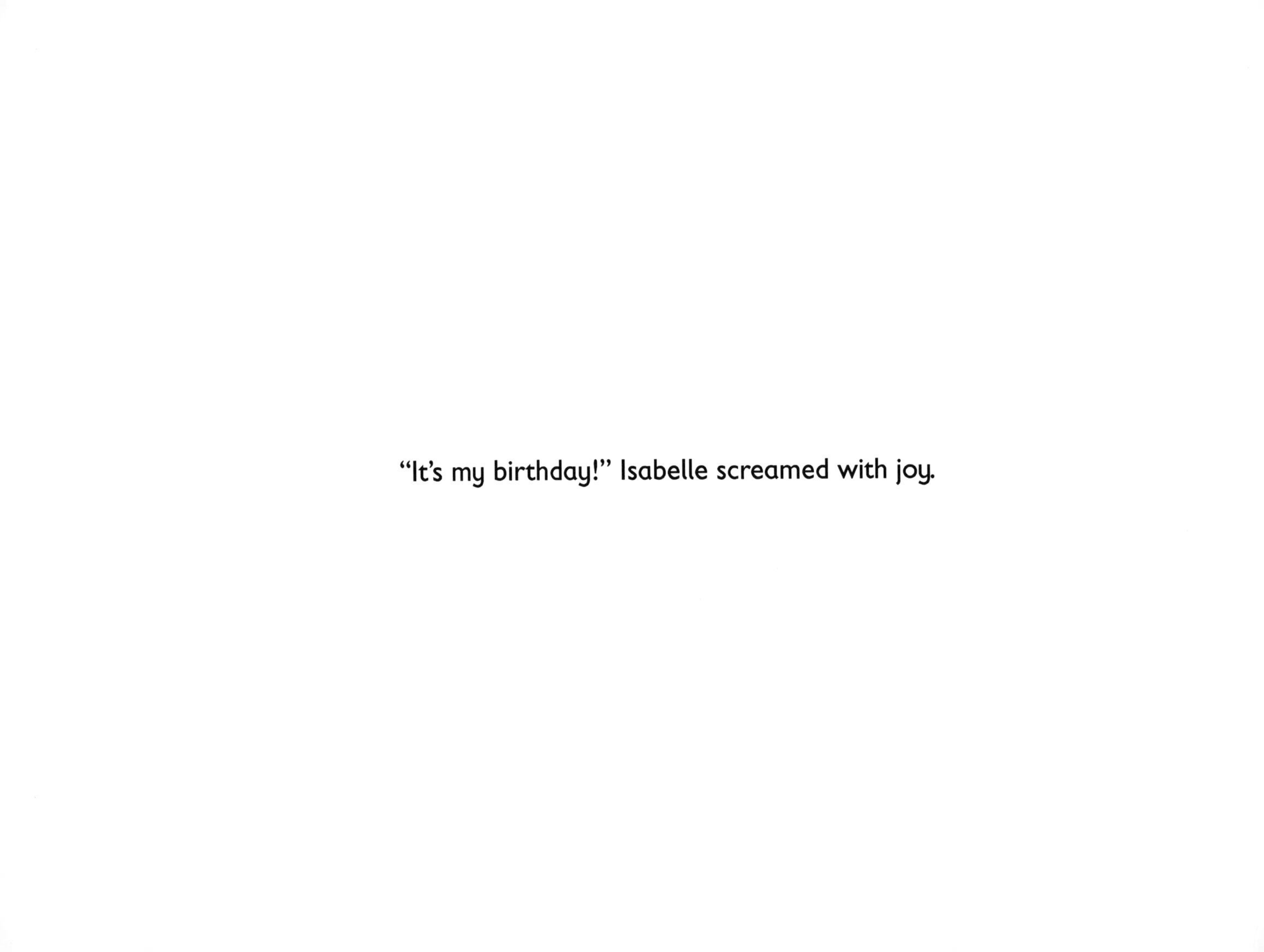

“It’s my birthday!” Isabelle screamed with joy.

IT'S MY
IRTHDAY!

Mommy had placed all of Isabelle's presents neatly in a pile in the corner of the room, next to a giant, pink balloon in the shape of a number eight. There was a pile of unopened envelopes filled with cards from loved ones.

"I want to open my cards first!" Isabelle said.

"Are you sure, Isabelle?" Mommy asked. Isabelle nodded and continued to pick up the pile of envelopes. She wanted this morning to last as long as it could. After all, she had waited patiently for this day, for such a long time.

Isabelle began opening all of her cards; she enjoyed reading all of the lovely messages from her friends and family. There was a card from Nanny and Grandad; there was a card from all of her aunts and uncles and even from all of her great grandparents!

Next, she found cards from her cousins and then cards from her friends from school. She was so happy. Finally, she got to the cards that were written to her from her younger brothers and last but not least, Mommy and Daddy.

"Are you ready for your presents now, Isabelle?" Daddy asked, who was almost as excited as Isabelle was, to see her open everything.

HAPPY
Birthday
TO YOU

“Yes, Daddy,” Isabelle replied excitedly and with the help of her brother, Noah, she began tearing away at the wrapping paper. Isabelle was so lucky this year, she had lots of new paints; she had a new doll that she had wanted for a long time.

There was also a really cool craft set that you could make your own puppets with. Isabelle loved making things.

She then noticed a large object that was covered by a sheet of wrapping paper; she could not tell what it was because it had not been wrapped into a shape she recognised. Slowly, she began to lift the paper away.

Paints

"It's a new bike!" Isabelle cried.

"You've outgrown your old bike, haven't you?" Mommy explained.

"Oh wow, I love it!" Isabelle said.

Mommy stood up and went to the window. She had one more surprise up her sleeve. She slowly opened the closed blinds to reveal the garden.

Towards the back of the garden was a large pink and purple bouncy castle. This time it was not only Isabelle who gasped in excitement, but her brother, Noah, stood with his mouth open, staring at the bouncy castle also.

"We're going to have a birthday party!" Mommy cried.

Before long, members of Isabelle's family started to arrive for the birthday party. Nanny and Grandad were very pleased to see her so happy.

"Did you like all of your presents, Isabelle?" Nanny asked.

"Yes, thank you, Nanny." Isabelle replied.

"You've been such a good girl." Grandad explained.

The party was now in full swing; Mommy was playing Isabelle's favourite music and there was party food and drinks filling the kitchen table, which was now in the garden. Balloons were everywhere and everyone was having a great time.

Some of the grown-ups were a little sad that they could not play on the bouncy castle however.

At the top of the garden, after playing on the bouncy castle, Isabelle stood and looked back down towards her house at her family, all having a good time.

She then realised that while she loved all of her presents, all of her cards, all of the balloons, all of the food and drink and of course the giant bouncy castle, none of it meant anything if it was not for her family being there on her special day. This made her smile.

Having a wonderful family like hers was the best present you could wish for. How lucky was she?

Suddenly, everyone went quiet. Mommy emerged from the back door holding a unicorn cake with eight candles lit. Isabelle and all of the other children rushed off the bouncy castle towards the house. It was time to sing happy birthday. Isabelle very quickly felt a bit shy, her cheeks went a lovely red colour and she could not stop smiling. Mommy leaned over to Isabelle with the birthday cake.

“Now make a wish.” Mommy said.

Isabelle closed her eyes, for quite a while actually; it must have been a big wish. Then she took a big breath and blew all of the candles out in one go. Last year, it took at least three attempts. Mommy then sliced the cake up into several pieces and everyone managed to grab a slice.

“Don’t forget to hand out your party bags.” Daddy said, handing Isabelle lots of little gift bags. Isabelle proceeded to hand them out to all of the children at the party. They all then rushed back on to the bouncy castle. Only this time, they were not alone.

The grown-ups could no longer hold in their excitement and all joined her on the bouncy castle. Everyone was having a great time. It was the best birthday party ever. Mommy leaned into Isabelle once more.

“What did you wish for, Isabelle?” Mommy asked quietly.

“If I told you that,” Isabelle explained, “It will never come true!”

Printed in Great Britain
by Amazon